Paddington
and the
Knickerbocker Rainbow

by Michael Bond
pictures by David McKee

G.P. Putnam's Sons
New York

One day Mr. Brown took Paddington and all
the family to the seashore for a treat.
Paddington sat in the front of the car with
Mr. and Mrs. Brown. Mrs. Bird, who looked
after them, sat in the back with Jonathan
and Judy.

But when they got to the seashore it was
raining hard and there was a gale blowing.
"Some treat!" said Mrs. Bird, as she held
on to her hat.

"Look!" cried Paddington. "That man's hair has blown away."

"Ssh!" hissed Judy. "He's bald."

But Paddington pulled his coat up
around his face. He didn't want his whiskers
to blow away.

"Let's go in here," said Mrs. Brown. "At least we shall be dry."

Paddington looked back at the sea. It was very rough.

"I think I shall put my arm bands on in case the tide comes in, and I need to float," he said.

As they sat down at a table, Mr. Brown pointed to a picture on the wall. It showed an ice cream called a Knickerbocker Glory.

"If you can say that, Paddington," he said, "I'll buy you one as a treat."

Paddington was very excited at the thought and he tried several times to say it.

"Knickernocker Glory . . . Gickerlocker Kory . . . Lickerlocker Rory . . ." But the more he tried the harder it was.

"I think I'll have an ice cream cone instead, Mr. Brown," he said sadly. "It isn't easy saying 'Knickerbocker Glory'."

Everybody laughed. And because in the end
Paddington had finally said it properly the waitress
brought him an extra large one on a tray.

"I couldn't get any more into the glass,"
she said.

Paddington licked his lips. "What a nice nurse!" he exclaimed.

"That wasn't a nurse," said Judy. "That was a waitress. Nurses look after people who are sick."

"If Paddington eats all that," said Jonathan, "he'll need a nurse."

Paddington gave Jonathan a hard stare. "Bears are good at eating ice cream," he said.

At that moment the sun came out. "I think it's going to be a nice day after all," said Mr. Brown. "Look – there's a rainbow."

"Quick, Paddington," said Mrs. Brown. "Look, before it goes away."

Paddington stared out of the window. He had never seen a rainbow before.

"It looks just like my Knickerbocker Glory," he said.

"And it disappears almost as quickly," said Mrs. Bird, as the rainbow began to fade.

"You must make a wish," said Judy, "before the rainbow goes."

"Then we can play on the beach," said Jonathan.

"I wish," said Paddington happily, "I wish I could have a Knickerbocker Rainbow every day of the week."